Rayne

Name:	Rayne
Age:	10
Height:	4'4"
Location:	The City
Hobbies:	Playing soccer, biking, gardening, growing vegetables, cooking with Grandpa Wyse, reading, playing piano, rock climbing
Favorite Snack:	Veggie pizza

MISSION

Lightning strikes Rayne's rooftop greenhouse! What will happen to her beloved vegetables?

SPROWTZ FILES

This book is dedicated to a future filled with healthy children.

THIS BOOK WAS PRINTED IN THE USA

Super Sprowtz™, ™, A Nutrition Education Series™, Rayne,

and all related titles, logos, and characters are trademarks of Super Sprowtz LLC.

Copyright © 2010 by Super Sprowtz LLC
Created by Radha Agrawal
Written by Radha Agrawal and Jessie Jenkins
Illustrations © 2010 by Super Sprowtz LLC
Illustrations by Archie Valdez
Cover art by Kenny Velez and Archie Valdez
Vegetable photography by Bill Levey
All Rights Reserved.

Published in the United States of America by
Super Sprowtz LLC, P.O. Box 500, New York, NY 10014

www.supersprowtz.com

ISBN-13 978-0-9844845-1-5 ISBN-10 0-9844845-1-5
WOR 10 9 8 7 6 5 4 3 2 1

green
circle
®
USA

ECO-FRIENDLY BOOKS
Made in the USA

THE SUPER SPROWTZ
ORIGINS

created by Radha Agrawal

written by Radha Agrawal and Jessie Jenkins
illustrated by Archie Valdez

This is Rayne, watering her garden.

Splish splash, splish splash.

She watches the water hit the leaves, trickle down the stems, and soak into the soil.

Trickle trickle, trickle trickle.

Grandpa Wyse stands by the door watching her proudly. He remembers the day Rayne asked him to build the greenhouse that now sparkles on their rooftop.

Sparkle sparkle, sparkle sparkle.

"Grandpa Wyse," she had said. "We have a great big roof but it's a sad and empty roof. Can't we build something sparkly and green?"

"I have an idea!" said Grandpa Wyse with a smile.

Grandpa Wyse and Rayne spent all spring planning and building their greenhouse. They called it the "Great Glass Greenhouse."

But this isn't a story about the Great Glass Greenhouse!

It's about the seeds that Rayne and Grandpa Wyse planted *in* the greenhouse. Rayne spent all summer watching the itty- bitty seeds grow into a rainbow of brightly colored vegetables!

Rayne loved her veggies so much that she even gave them names.

She named her reddest tomato Todd Tomato, her orangest carrot
Colby Carrot, her purplest eggplant Erica Eggplant,
and she named all her other vegetables too!

She even made up *songs* for them!

"I love you Ms. Eggplant,
You're the smartest of plants,
So I'm calling you Erica,
And together we'll dance!"

One day, as Rayne was watering her plant friends, splishing and splashing, she heard a *Crack! Crash! Boom!* Suddenly, the clouds turned from a marshmallowy white to a menacing gray.

Uh oh.

Crack! Crash! Boom!

Rayne ran for cover as fast as her legs would carry her.
She had just reached the stairwell when a huge bolt
of lightning struck the Great Glass Greenhouse.

Oh no! What would happen to her vegetables?

Rayne's eyes were as wide as frisbees
as she watched the Great Glass Greenhouse
being struck over and over again
by lightning.

When the storm finally stopped, it looked like a million fireflies
were buzzing around the shattered greenhouse.

"What's happening?" she wondered.

Rayne tiptoed back to the greenhouse. *Tip toe, tip toe.*

She crossed her fingers and closed her eyes as she inched closer and closer, hoping her favorite sprouts - her friends - were okay.

Well, you shouldn't cross your fingers and close your eyes while tiptoeing! Rayne stumbled and flew through the greenhouse door.

Trrippp! Crash! Boom!

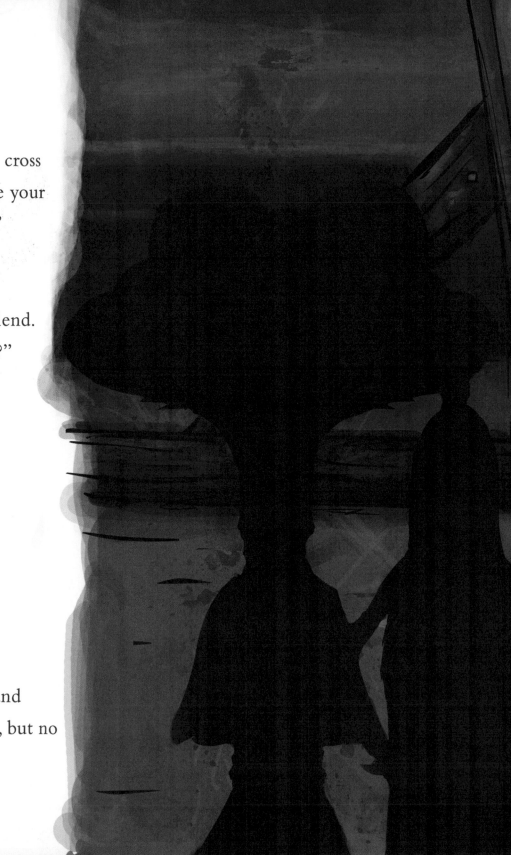

Silence. And then...

"You really shouldn't cross your fingers and close your eyes while tiptoeing," she heard a voice say.

"Be nice, she's our friend. Are you okay, Rayne?" she heard another voice say.

Rayne looked up and opened her mouth, but no words came out.

"Are you okay Rayne?" It was, if you can believe it, a talking broccoli wearing a striped jumpsuit! He had really big muscles...for a broccoli.

Gulp. Rayne swallowed.

"Don't be afraid, Rayne. We're your friends."

This time, the voice was coming from her favorite eggplant, who was wearing really enormous eyeglasses...for an eggplant.

Rayne finally found her voice. "W-who are you?"

She looked around and realized that she was surrounded by *all* her favorite vegetables, but now they had arms and legs and were wearing funny outfits!

"Why Rayne, don't you recognize us? You gave us our names!
You splish-splashed water on us every day!

My name is Erica Eggplant!"

Erica? That was the name *she* had given
her beautiful eggplant!

Her vegetables had magically come to life!

"You must be Brian Broccoli!" she exclaimed, pointing at the muscular-looking broccoli. Brian Broccoli flexed his arms and smiled.

"And you're Colby Carrot!" Colby Carrot beamed at her through his golden mask.

A tall and leafy spinach held out his hand in greeting. Rayne rubbed her eyes in disbelief – she could have sworn his arm grew longer as he reached up towards her.

"I am Sammy Spinach and I am Super Stretchy! We are the Super Sprowtz, Rayne, and we are here to protect the City."

The super what?!

But before Rayne could ask
any questions, Erica Eggplant
clapped her hands together
- *clap clap* - and said,
"Okay, Super Sprowtz, let's
get to work!"

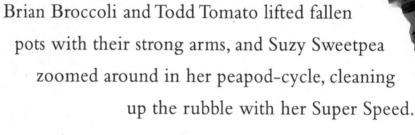

Every one of the Sprowtz
sprang into action!

Brian Broccoli and Todd Tomato lifted fallen
pots with their strong arms, and Suzy Sweetpea
zoomed around in her peapod-cycle, cleaning
up the rubble with her Super Speed.

Zoom zoom, zoom zoom!

Zach Zucchini made sure all the plants were watered while Miki Mushroom repaired their broken stalks and torn leaves. Sammy Spinach reached his arms to the ceiling and fixed all the broken glass while Oliver Onion and Gita Garlic teamed up to sweep the floor.

Minutes, seconds and milliseconds later, the Great Glass Greenhouse
was back up and running again!

As Rayne walked around in awe,
she noticed one thing
that was a *little* different...

Grandpa Wyse's toolshed, damaged by the
storm, was put back together - trim and tidy
as ever. But now, at the bottom of the door,
just about eggplant height, hung a little sign
that read "Super Sprowtz HQ."

Rayne looked down at the sign
and exclaimed, "I can't wait to
introduce you to Grandpa Wyse!"

Erica Eggplant responded somewhat sternly, "Rayne, only you
can know we exist! I'm afraid grownups just don't get it."

Rayne frowned and said, "But your headquarters are in
Grandpa Wyse's toolshed! Won't he see you?"

Erica Eggplant opened the door to the shed, revealing a curious
rabbit hole in the back wall. "Super Sprowtz!" she ordered. "To your stations!"

One by one, the Super Sprowtz disappeared into the rabbit hole. Rayne got down on her hands and knees to follow them but could barely fit her head inside the door – it was perfectly Sprowtz-sized!

The Super Sprowtz were in an enormous room filled with computers, gadgets and contraptions. In the middle of the room hovered an image of a sinister man surrounded by wisps of dirty smoke.

"What is this place?" Rayne marveled. "And WHO is that?"

"*This* is the Super Sprowtz Headquarters," replied Erica Eggplant. "And *that* is Pompous Pollution. He is in charge of a gang of real troublemakers."

"Troublemakers?" asked Rayne.

"Don't worry," said Erica Eggplant, "we'll be keeping an eye on them from here!"

Rayne was bursting with questions but knew they would have to wait for another day. She headed back downstairs. It was time for a bubble bath anyway.

What adventures lie in store for Rayne and the Super Sprowtz?

Hey Super Parents!

Rayne's adventures with the Super Sprowtz are just beginning and so are your adventures in the kitchen with your kids! Kids love pizza and it can be a great way to encourage them to try new vegetables. Don't worry if you're not up for making homemade pizza dough (although we tried it and it wasn't as hard as we thought!) - it's easy to find pre-made crusts at the grocery store. Just be sure to check the ingredients and avoid those that contain partially-hydrogenated oil.

Get your kids involved in making pizza too - have them use different colored veggies to make smiley faces or other shapes on their pizza!

Happy Cooking!

Love, *Grandpa Wyse* & *Rayne*

Grandpa Wyse's Super Veggie Pizza

Serves: 2 adults or 4 kids   Time: 20 minutes (+ 2-3 hours if making your own dough)
Level: Easy if you buy the crust. Medium if you make your own!

1 pre-made whole wheat pizza crust or homemade dough (see next page)
1/2 cup tomato sauce
Your choice of veggies! Ideas include:

- steamed or roasted broccoli
- sliced zucchini
- fresh tomatoes
- roasted eggplant
- thinly sliced red onion
- sliced mushrooms

Organic mozzarella cheese (fresh or regular) - as much or as little as you like!
Salt and pepper to taste

Preheat oven to 500°F. Lay the crust out on a flat surface. If you are using homemade dough, roll out the dough on a lightly floured board. Top the crust evenly with the sauce. Top the sauce with your choice of veggies. Top veggies with cheese - shredded if you use regular mozzarella, thinly sliced if you use fresh. Season with a little salt and pepper.

Place the pizza on a baking sheet or pizza stone and place in the oven. Cook for about 10 minutes or until the crust is brown and crispy. Let pizza cool slightly, slice and enjoy!

Super Pizza Dough

1 pack of active dry yeast
3/4 cup warm water (115°F)
1 tbsp extra virgin olive oil
1 3/4 cup bread flour or unbleached all-purpose flour
1/2 tsp sugar
1 tsp salt

In a small mixing bowl, whisk together yeast, warm water, sugar and olive oil. Let sit for about 3 minutes to fully dissolve and activate the yeast.
In a large mixing bowl, whisk together flour and salt.
With a rubber spatula, gradually mix the yeast mixture into the flour until just combined and dough barely holds together. Turn the dough out onto a clean counter surface dusted with flour.

Knead the dough with some extra flour until the dough has become smooth and elastic, about 10 minutes. The surface should be tight and silky. Lightly grease a large mixing bowl with olive oil and place the dough in it. Cover the bowl tightly with plastic wrap and set in a warm place to rise until doubled in size, about 1 to 2 hours.

Once the dough has doubled, punch it down and divide it into 2 equal sized pieces. Knead each piece to form a uniform ball. Set dough aside and cover with a kitchen towel or plastic wrap to rest for 30 minutes. After 30 minutes, the dough is ready to be rolled out, topped with sauce, veggies and cheese, and baked. If you only need one crust, freeze the second one for another night!

View how-to video and post your favorite cooking pictures at supersprowtz.com!

Special thanks to Super Chef Chris Sorensen for his Super Pizza Dough recipe! For more of Chef Chris's delicious, kid-friendly recipes, visit supersprowtz.com.

BROCCOLI - SUPER STRONG

A Super Food! Full of nutrients, antioxidants and vitamins including A, K, and immune system-boosting vitamin C. Also contains calcium, which is important for strong bones and phytonutrients which may have anti-cancer effects.

CARROTS - SUPER SIGHT

Rich in beta-carotene, which the body converts to vitamin A. Vitamin A promotes good vision – especially at night!

EGGPLANT - SUPER SMART

Purple and blue vegetables and fruits like eggplant have phytochemicals that are good for memory. Eggplant also contains nasunin, which protects brain cell membranes. Eggplant is rich in antioxidants that can reduce the risk of cancer.

PEAS - SUPER SPEED

Contain lots of vitamins and minerals, as well as dietary fiber and protein. Green peas are a great source of energy!

ONION AND GARLIC - SUPER SWEET

Both contain sulfides, which may lower blood lipids and blood pressure and help protect against heart disease.

ZUCCHINI - SUPER SWIMMER

Full of water, zucchini also contains folate and other B vitamins, which have numerous health benefits, including lowering bad cholesterol and improving lipid profiles.

SPINACH - SUPER STRETCHY

Packed with nutrients, spinach is a rich source of vitamins A and K and many antioxidants, as well as minerals such as calcium, magnesium, manganese and iron.

TOMATO - SUPER SAFE

Technically a fruit, tomatoes contain significant amounts of vitamin C and lycopene, which have antioxidant and cancer-preventing properties.

MUSHROOMS - SUPER SOOTHING

These members of the fungi kingdom provide a significant amount of potassium, a mineral that helps the body maintain normal heart rhythm, fluid balance and muscle function.

Please note, never let your child eat mushrooms they find in the wild! Only experts can distinguish edible mushrooms from poisonous ones.

For more information, visit supersprowtz.com!

RADHA AGRAWAL

Radha is the creator of Super Sprowtz. She passionately believes that the current conversation with children about food isn't working. After opening Slice, an organic pizzeria, with her twin sister, Radha became a regular visitor to New York City public schools where she spoke about nutrition and healthy living. Alarmed by what she saw as a growing obesity epidemic among urban children, she became deeply committed to changing the way children eat. This, combined with her years of experience in story-telling as a commercial and film producer led her to create the Super Sprowtz. It is her belief that through entertaining story lines, catchy music, and lovable characters, children can see vegetables and nutrition differently. She earned her Bachelor of Science degree from Cornell University where she also played Varsity soccer. She currently lives, paints, bikes and eats locally (likely at Slice) in New York City.

JESSIE JENKINS

Jessie brings her love for healthy eating, her belief in sustainable food systems and her commitment to education to Super Sprowtz. Born and raised in New York City, Jessie taught ninth-grade science in Manhattan's Washington Heights, a neighborhood where 95% of the students qualify for the city's free-lunch program and 21% of adults are obese. While teaching, she created and fully funded the Learning Garden project - a rooftop classroom where teachers integrated gardening into their curricula. Jessie holds a BA in Environmental Studies from Oberlin College and a Masters in Science Education from Teachers College Columbia University. She lives and gardens in Brooklyn, New York.

ARCHIE P. VALDEZ

Archie P. Valdez has created art for video games, books, graphic novels, animations and commercials. Originally from the Philippines, Archie was raised in Nigeria before moving to the U.S. He studied art in San Francisco at the Academy of Art University, where he earned his Bachelor of Fine Arts with a focus in animation and illustration. Archie was initially a music and chemistry major and is still passionate about those fields - you can hear him singing sometimes when he works. Archie likes to travel, cook (in moderation), play video games and various sports, and drink coffee while sketching. He also loves to watch cartoons. Archie lives in New York City. He loves finding delicious snacks to munch on at the Farmer's Market in Union Square.

Now Available

The Super Sprowtz: Origins!

I Am Brian Broccoli and I Am Super Strong!

I Am Erica Eggplant and I Am Super Smart!

Coming Soon

I Am Colby Carrot and I Have Super Sight!

I Am Suzy Sweetpea and I Have Super Speed!

I Am Todd Tomato and I Am Super Safe!

I Am Miki Mushroom and I Am Super Soothing!

I Am Sammy Spinach and I Am Super Stretchy!

I Am Zach Zucchini and I Am a Super Swimmer!

We Are Oliver Onion and Gita Garlic and We Are Super Sweet!

For more information
visit us at
supersprowtz.com